V&J Gordon Memorial Library

T 623753

D1312203

VIRGIL AND JOSEPHINE GORDON
MEMORIAL LIBRARY
917 North Circle Drive
SEALY, TEXAS 77474

VIRGIE AND JOSEPHINE GORDON
MEMORIAL LIBRARY
917 North Circle Drive
SEALY, TEXAS 77474

AMERICAN FOOTBALL CONFERENCE

Buffalo Bill
Buffalo Bills

Benny Bengal
Cincinnati Bengals

Brownie Brown
Cleveland Browns

Bucky Bronco
Denver Broncos

Oscar Oiler
Houston Oilers

Cody Colt
Indianapolis Colts

Casey Chief
Kansas City Chiefs

Rip Raider
Los Angeles Raiders

Dolph Dolphin
Miami Dolphins

Pat Patriot
New England Patriots

Jumbo Jet
New York Jets

Stevie Steeler
Pittsburgh Steelers

Charlie Charger
San Diego Chargers

Sandy Seahawk
Seattle Seahawks

All Huddles Characters; TM and © 1983 NFL Properties, Inc. All rights reserved.

Text and illustrations © 1984 Parker Brothers, Division of CPG Products, Corp. All rights reserved.

Library of Congress Cataloging in Publication Data. Havel, Jennifer. The wacky rulebook. (The Huddles) SUMMARY: Since the Huddles always follow the rules given them by the Coach, Charlie Cheater decides to confuse them by substituting a new rule book while the Coach is away. 1. Children's stories, American.
[1. Behavior—Fiction] I. Ewers, Joe, ill. II. Title. III. Series.
PZ7.H294Cr 1984 [E] 84-1149 ISBN 0-910313-77-6
Manufactured in the United States of America   1 2 3 4 5 6 8 9 0   01

The Wacky Rulebook

Story by Jennifer Havel
Pictures by Joe Ewers

With Special Thanks to Steve Lavers and John Carrozza

CHILDRENS PRESS CHOICE
A Parker Brothers title selected for educational distribution
ISBN 0-516-09043-7

In the land of Huddlestown lived
twenty-eight friendly, fun-loving Huddles
and their Coach. The Huddles played hard and
worked hard. The Coach trained the Huddles
to be strong and healthy and to play fair.

Sometimes the Huddles grumbled because
the Coach was strict. But he only wanted
them to be the very best Huddles they could
be. So whenever the Coach left town, even for
a few days, he left behind his rulebook in case
the Huddles had any problems.

One week the Coach was away, and
everything was going very smoothly. Jumbo
Jet was cruising above Huddlestown. He liked
to keep an eye on the town and see what
Chuck Cheater was up to. Chuck and his
gang lived in Out of Bounds on the outskirts
of town. Chuck did not get along with the
Huddles because the Huddles always played
by the rules, and all Chuck cared about was
winning any way he could.

"Well, everything looks fine to me," said Jumbo, as he headed back to his hangar in Huddlestown.

But everything wasn't fine at all. Hidden from Jumbo's sight, under some thick bushes, Chuck Cheater was talking to his three gang members, Sydney Sneak, Kevin Kick, and Martin Fumble.

"It makes me sick!" groaned Chuck.
"Those Huddles are doing just what they are
supposed to do even though the Coach is
away. I can't stand it anymore! Luckily, I
think I have a way to mess up Huddlestown
for good!"

"How, Chuck?" asked Sydney.

"The Coach is gone for a week, right? And
don't the Huddles always play by the rules?"

"Always," agreed Martin.

"And don't the Huddles always do what
the Coach tells them?"

"Always," groaned Kevin.

"Well, I have made up a phony list of rules for the Huddles. Huddlestown will be so messed up when they follow these rules that they will have to call it Muddlestown!"

"Great thinking, Chuck! But how will you get the Huddles to follow the phony rules?" asked Sydney.

Chuck smiled a crooked smile. "That's where you come in, Sydney...."

The next morning, the Huddles woke up
early and did their exercises. Later on, they
gathered in the clubhouse for lunch.

The doorbell to the clubhouse rang. It was
Sydney Sneak disguised as a mail carrier.

When Cowboy Joe answered the door,
Sydney handed him a thick white envelope.
"Special Delivery," he said.

"Thank you," said Cowboy Joe. "Wow! It's
from the Coach. It must be important."

Inside the envelope was a letter and a big list. Cowboy Joe read the letter out loud:

Cowboy Joe held up the list. "Well, here goes," he said.

    1. Walk on your hands for the first ten minutes of each hour. Then hop on one leg for the next ten minutes.

2. Dolph Dolphin: Teach Sandy Seahawk, Ernie Eagle, and Freddie Falcon how to swim.

3. Reddy Redskin and Rip Raider: Take turns teaching Dolph Dolphin how to fly.

4. Cowboy Joe: Leave your rope on the highest branch of the tallest tree in Huddlestown.

5. Jumbo Jet: Practice floating on the river.

6. All Huddles: Remove one object from another Huddle's home.

"What!" cried all the Huddles. "The Coach must be joking!"

"We can't swim!" cried Sandy, Ernie, and Freddie.

"I can't fly!" cried Dolph.

"Why would I want to know how to float?" complained Jumbo.

"Take each other's things! This is impossible!" cried the Huddles.

"You know what the Coach says," Cowboy Joe reminded everyone. "Nothing is impossible if you try hard enough."

Although Cowboy Joe didn't understand
the new rules either, he said, "Let's get
started. Maybe the rules will make more sense
as we go along. It's just three o'clock now.
Let's start walking on our hands."

The Huddles all got up on their hands.
They fell down steps, bumped into each other,
and landed in a big pile. It was a mess!

After bandaging their scuffed knees, they
all began to hop around. They couldn't get
any of their chores done, and they grew tired
very fast.

That night, the Huddles went to bed upset
and sore.

The next day was even worse!

Cowboy Joe got up early and found the
tallest tree in Huddlestown. He climbed to the
very top and wrapped his rope around the
highest branch.

"This certainly does seem strange to me,"
he muttered, as he climbed down the tree.

He walked over to Big Red Cardinal's treehouse, which was nearby. No one was home, so he slipped in through a window and slipped out with one of Big Red's helmets.

"And this doesn't make me feel good at all!" he said to himself, as he walked home.

Dolph Dolphin led Sandy Seahawk, Ernie Eagle, and Freddie Falcon down to his houseboat to try to teach them to swim in his pool. Sandy's turn was first.

"Brrrrr. This is cold," complained Sandy. "I don't know where on earth the Coach got the idea that flyers should also be swimmers!"

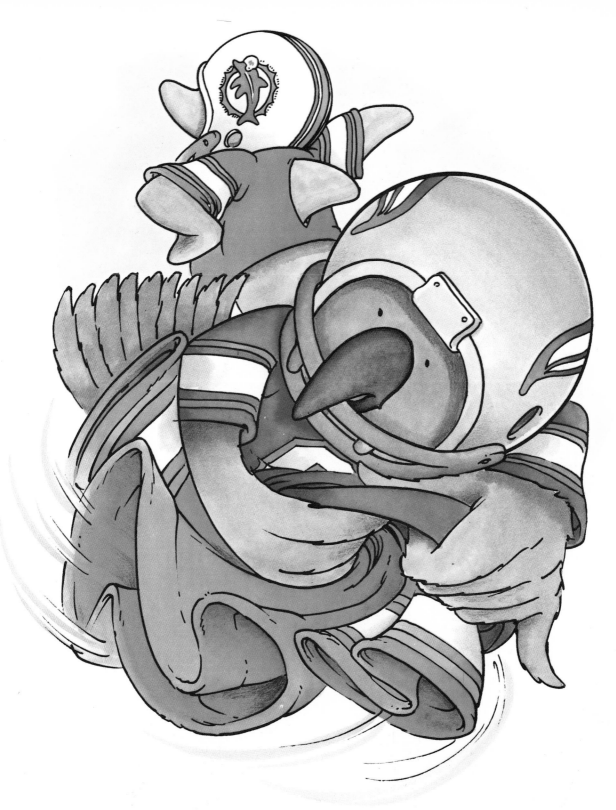

When Dolph wasn't looking, Sandy
grabbed one of Dolph's blue jerseys and
stuffed it under his own.

After having no luck with Ernie or Freddie either, Dolph decided to give up for the day. The pool was covered with feathers and the Huddles were shivering with the cold. Dolph was discouraged, and now it was time for his flying lesson.

On the way to his lesson, Dolph walked into Jumbo's hangar and took a pair of Jumbo's flying goggles. ''Guess I can use these for swimming,'' he thought to himself.

When Dolph got to the playing field, Rip Raider and Reddy Redskin were already there. Dolph lay down on the field and the other Huddles called encouragement to him.

"Wave your flippers, Dolph!" they shouted. Then they stood on either side of him and helped him up. He waved his flippers. But when they let him go, he dropped to the ground.

"Ugh!" moaned Dolph.

Huddlestown was in a real muddle!

Chuck Cheater was hiding near the river talking to Martin Fumble and Sydney Sneak.

"Didn't I tell you Huddlestown would never be the same? And we don't have to worry about Jumbo Jet spying on us anymore. He'll be sunk very soon. And Kevin Kick is getting Cowboy Joe's rope down from the tree this very minute. So Cowboy Joe won't be able to rescue Jumbo!"

But Chuck didn't count on the Coach arriving home a day early. When the Coach strolled into Huddlestown, his mouth dropped open. Everywhere Huddles were walking on their hands! The Coach opened the clubhouse door just as Stevie Steeler was coming out, upside down! Stevie fell. And the Coach fell on top of him!

"What is going on here?" shouted the Coach.

"Sorry, Coach," said Stevie. "The new rules you sent are really tough. I'm on my way to Packy's house now to steal his favorite mixing bowl."

"What new rules? I didn't send any new rules! You know stealing is wrong. Where's Cowboy Joe?" demanded the Coach.

"He's down by the river helping Jumbo Jet
learn how to float."

"He's doing what?" cried the Coach. "Stay
right where you are. I have to run down to
the river. We'll all talk about this later." He
ran off.

Just as the Coach got to the river, Jumbo
started to sink. "Help!" cried Jumbo. "I
can't float!"

"Cowboy Joe, come quick!" called the
Coach. "Pull Jumbo out with your rope!"

"My rope is at the top of the tallest tree, just where you wanted it," answered Cowboy Joe.

"Oh, no! What on earth is going on here!" cried the Coach.

Luckily, Dolph Dolphin had returned to his houseboat and was swimming in his pool. He heard all the shouting. He swam over to Jumbo as fast as he could and dove underneath him.

When Dolph came up again, he was carrying Jumbo safely on his back.

''I've got him now!'' Dolph cried to everyone on the shore.

All the Huddles began jumping up and down with excitement. They were so glad Jumbo was safe.

"Thank you so much, Dolph," said Jumbo,
after he had caught his breath. "I think I've
figured out why we're all in such a muddle.
When I was out in the river, I saw a certain
sneaky person hiding in those bushes over
there, practicing rope tricks with Cowboy
Joe's rope!"

Chuck Cheater was trying to do a trick when he heard his name. He tried to drop the rope and run. As if by magic, the rope wrapped itself around Chuck's feet. Before long he was all tangled up. He pulled on both ends, but that only made it worse.

"Yikes!" cried Chuck. "I'm stuck!"

"Yippee!" cried Cowboy Joe. He untied his rope from around Chuck's feet, made a loop and tossed it over Chuck just as that sneak was trying to get away again.

"I think I understand where the new rules came from now," said the Coach. "What's your hurry, Chuck? You and your gang have work to do. Stevie Steeler told me the new rules asked the Huddles to take things that didn't belong to them. Well, Chuck, why don't you and your gang spend the rest of the day returning the 'borrowed' objects? That should keep you out of trouble for a while."

"Hurray!" shouted all the Huddles.

"You also have work to do, Huddles," said the Coach. "I want things back in shape in a jiffy. And when you're through, run three extra laps just for good measure."

The Huddles smiled at each other. They were glad things were back to normal again.

"Welcome home, Coach," they said, as they set to work.

44

NATIONAL FOOTBALL CONFERENCE

Freddie Falcon
Atlanta Falcons

Buddy Bear
Chicago Bears

Cowboy Joe
Dallas Cowboys

Leo Lion
Detroit Lions

Packy Packer
Green Bay Packers

Ramsey Ram
Los Angeles Rams

Victor Viking
Minnesota Vikings

Sir Saint
New Orleans Saints

Jolly Giant
New York Giants

Ernie Eagle
Philadelphia Eagles

Big Red
St. Louis Cardinals

Niner 49er
San Francisco 49ers

Buckles Buc
Tampa Bay Buccaneers

Reddy Redskin
Washington Redskins